D1360262

The Enchanted Castle

E. Nesbit

Adapted by Lesley Sims

Illustrated by Alan Marks

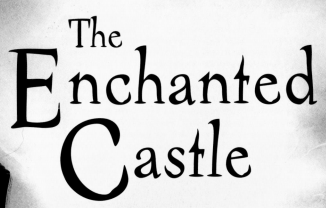

Reading Consultant: Alison Kelly
Roehampton University

Contents

Chapter 1
Exploring

"This is the most boring summer ever," said Gerald, looking at Cathy and Jimmy's glum faces. Their parents were abroad and they had been left to stay with Marie, an old friend of their mother's.

"We need an adventure," he said.

"You can't just *have* an adventure," said Jimmy, who liked to disagree with everyone.

"But you can look for one," Gerald replied firmly. "Let's go exploring. I'll ask Marie if we can."

"Like that?" asked Cathy.

Gerald glanced in the mirror. His hair was sticking up and he had a blob of strawberry jam on his chin. "Perhaps I'll clean up first."

4

Minutes later, he went to the sitting room. "I've been thinking," he began. "Wouldn't it be easier for you if we went out during the day?"

Marie smiled. "You mean you want to explore," she said. "Of course. Why not take a picnic?"

Everyone felt more cheerful as they left the house. It was certainly a good day for exploring. The street lay bathed in sunshine and dust sparkled in the road like diamonds.

"My friend told me there was an enchanted castle near here," said Gerald, as they strode along the hot, dusty road.

"Enchanted?" mocked Jimmy. "What an idiot. But a castle might be fun," he added. "Where is it?"

Gerald shrugged. "No idea." He stopped as they reached a fork in the road.

"Let's try this one," Cathy said, taking the right-hand fork.

"It must be lunchtime now," said
Jimmy, after a while. So they sat
by a hedge to eat the picnic.

Gerald finished first and leaned
back against the hedge, which
promptly gave way. "Hey!" he
cried, as he disappeared down
a hole.

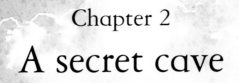

Chapter 2
A secret cave

A breathless pause followed. "Are you alright?" asked Jimmy.

"Yes," Gerald called. "And guess what? I've found a cave!"

Cathy climbed in, dry leaves rustling under her boots. Jimmy followed, diving head first.

"Follow me," said Gerald, who had discovered a passageway.

One by one, they crept along, coming out through an arch into brilliant sunshine.

"Oh!" breathed Cathy. "Is it the enchanted castle?"

They were on a marble terrace overlooking a lake. Creamy white statues dotted the grounds and up ahead rose the turrets and towers of a castle. A sense of magic hung in the air.

The place was deserted. As they walked, the feeling of magic grew stronger. They halted at the start of a maze. "I bet there's something magical in the middle," said Gerald. But the middle was hard to find.

They were back at the start for the fourth time when Gerald spotted a thread of cotton, tied to a silver thimble engraved with a crown.

"It's a clue!" he cried.

The clue wound around the
hedges, across a grassy plot and
stopped at a small hand. The hand
belonged to someone in a long silk
gown and a glittering veil, who
was fast asleep in the sun.

"Sleeping Beauty..." Cathy whispered. "You're the eldest, Gerry. Kiss her awake."

"Never!" cried Gerald, alarmed.

"*I* will," said Jimmy and planted a loud kiss on her pale cheek.

The Princess opened her eyes, yawned and said, "The hundred years must be over. Do you want to come to my castle for tea?"

14

They followed the Princess into a magnificent hall and sat down at a long oak table. All three were now convinced they had found an enchanted place. So it was a shock when they were only offered bread and cheese to eat.

"Well, Cook *has* been asleep for a hundred years..." said the Princess.

"Now," she went on, "you can see my treasures." She took them to an empty room. A blazing oblong of light filled the room with sunshine. "This is my treasure chamber."

"But where," asked Cathy politely, "*are* the treasures?"

The Princess made them shut their eyes and they heard a click.

"You may look," she said and they looked, amazed. Shelves ran around the room, filled with sparkling jewels.

16

Then Cathy noticed a brooch, and a ring made of a dull metal. "What are these?" she asked.

"Don't touch!" cried the Princess. "They're magic."

"The brooch will give me any wish I like. The ring makes me invisible," she added.

"Could you give us a wish?" asked Gerald.

"No," said the Princess firmly, "but I'll become invisible for you."

"Shut your eyes, count to fifty and look," she ordered. "Then close them and count to fifty again."

On 'fifty' they opened their eyes. The Princess had gone.

After counting to fifty a second time, they looked again. There was no sign of her.

"It's just a trick," said Jimmy. "She must be hiding."

"Please come back," said Cathy.

"Don't be silly!" said the voice of the Princess, sounding angry.

"What's the matter?" Gerald asked the air. "You said you'd be invisible and you are."

"I *was* hiding," snapped the voice. "But now I'm here, so stop pretending."

"But we're not pretending," Gerald said. "Look in the mirror."

"Oh – OH! I *am* invisible. What shall I do?" wailed the voice.

"Take the ring off," said Cathy.

"I-I *can't*! It's stuck."

Chapter 3
Invisible!

Sobbing filled the room. "What shall I do?" wept the voice. "I'm not really a princess. I dressed up for fun. My aunt is Lord Yalding's housekeeper. He owns this castle. I'm only Mabel Prowse."

They wandered outside, trying
to decide what to do.

"Your shadow's not invisible
anyway," Jimmy observed.

"Who cares about my shadow?"
said Mabel's voice.

"I think you should stay with us
until this is fixed," said Gerald.
"You'd better leave a note for your
aunt so she doesn't worry."

22

Since Mabel was invisible, it was easy to get her into Marie's house without anyone noticing.

The next day, Mabel pretended the bedsheets were haunted, terrifying Eliza the maid.

"That was fun," Mabel's voice told the others. "What shall we do now? I know!" she added, seconds later. "Let's go to the fair."

"Gerry can pretend to do magic," she explained. "Of course, I'll be doing it really."

Seated on a mat, with a scarf tied around his head like a turban, Gerald looked very impressive.

"Ladies and gentlemen!" he cried. "Prepare for genuine magic."

Scornful laughter broke out, but then Gerald began. Hats danced in the air and coins disappeared.

"For my final trick," Gerald declared, "*I* shall disappear!" He planned to hide under Mabel's invisible veil, which he hoped would act like a cloak of invisibility.

But it didn't work. The audience moved closer, sounding angry.

As Gerald began to panic, Mabel hissed in his ear, "The ring's loose!"

Quickly, she ducked behind a tent, took off the ring and rolled it to him. Gerald stood up, bowed, put on the ring – and vanished.

The others were waiting behind
a tent, when they heard Gerald's
voice. "Hello," he said miserably.

"Oh!" said Mabel. "You made
me jump. I have to get home," she
added. "Take the ring off now."

"*I can't!*" said the voice.

Mabel frowned. "Well, I have
to go," she said again. "My aunt
will be wondering where I am."

"I may as well come with you,"
the invisible Gerald offered. "I
can hardly go to Marie's like this.
Cathy and Jimmy can tell her I've
gone to bed with a headache."

Back at the castle, the invisible Gerald left Mabel to find her aunt and wandered around the grounds. A silent white figure slipped by a weeping willow and danced past.

Gerald was puzzled until he saw an empty pedestal. "Can the statues come to *life*?" he wondered, astonished.

A stone dinosaur lumbered past, catching Gerald's hand with its tail. Gerald felt a sudden terror and fled.

It was very late by the time he finally arrived home and crept into bed. He was so tired he didn't even notice the magic had worn off and he was no longer invisible.

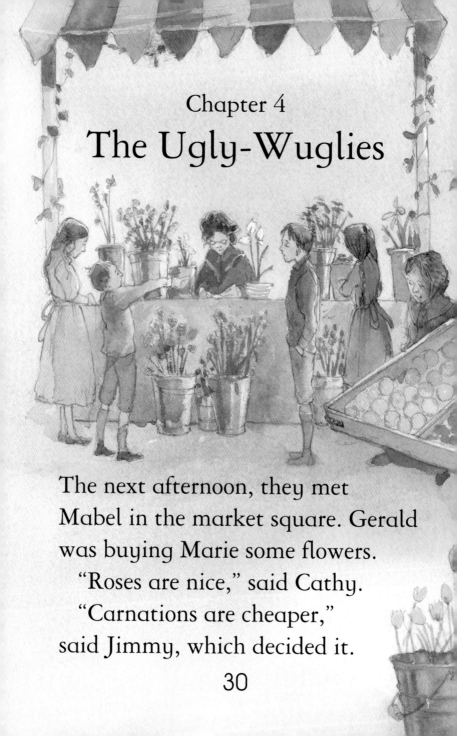

Chapter 4
The Ugly-Wuglies

The next afternoon, they met
Mabel in the market square. Gerald
was buying Marie some flowers.

"Roses are nice," said Cathy.

"Carnations are cheaper,"
said Jimmy, which decided it.

Marie was in her sitting room, drawing a picture of the castle.

"Oh!" said Mabel. "That's Yalding Towers. That's where I live."

Marie looked shocked. "You are Lord Yalding's daughter?"

"Oh no," said Mabel. "He doesn't have a family. I'm the housekeeper's niece. Lord Yalding's too poor to live there. He inherited the castle without any money." Mabel paused for breath. "It's a very sad story."

"He fell in love with a poor girl his uncle didn't think was suitable and he wanted to punish him, so he left all the money to his cousins. Then *her* relatives sent her to a convent and Lord Yalding couldn't find her." Mabel sighed.

Marie looked thoughtful.

"I almost forgot," said Gerald, holding out the flowers. "These are for you."

"You dear children!" Marie cried. "Your friend must stay for tea. I shall buy cakes." Smiling at the children, she left.

After tea, they decided to put
on a play for Marie and Eliza –
and six very strange guests.

Marie stared at them. "Oh!" she
gasped. "They're not real."

"They're Ugly-Wuglies," Jimmy
explained. "We made them for
an audience."

"Beauty and the Beast!" shouted
a voice and the play began.

Finally, it was time for the Beast
to let Beauty visit her family.

"Farewell," said Gerald the Beast
to Mabel. "Take this ring with
you. It's a magic wishing ring."

Mabel put it on as Marie and Eliza clapped politely. It was the ring from the castle.

"I wish the Ugly-Wuglies were alive," she muttered. "We'd get proper applause then."

To Gerald's horror, a padded clapping sound began and, one by one, the Ugly-Wuglies turned their heads to look at them.

Eliza and Marie fled with loud shrieks. The children yanked the curtain across the stage as Gerald grabbed the ring.

"It must be a wishing ring now," he said. "I wish the Uglies-Wuglies weren't alive!" he added and peered around the curtain. The creatures were more alive than ever.

"A oo re o me a oo ho el?" one asked. Gerald finally realized that the monster was asking, "Can you recommend a good hotel?"

Gerald ducked behind the curtain. "Cheer up," he told the others, trying to sound brave. "Being invisible didn't last. Maybe this won't. We just need to hide them till it wears off."

"There's a temple in the castle grounds..." suggested Mabel.

"Perfect," said Gerald. "Cathy, will you tell Marie I'm walking Mabel home? Say the Uglies were just a trick we did with strings."

Jimmy looked relieved he and Cathy weren't going as well. "They give me the shivers," he said.

37

Mabel sighed with relief when they finally ushered the Ugly-Wuglies into the temple and directed them to a passage through a door at the back.

"It leads to a good hotel," she said, with her fingers crossed.

"Thank goodness that's over," she went on, as they slammed the door behind the last Ugly-Wugly.

"What's over?" demanded a voice and she jumped.

A man was watching them.

"You won't believe it," said Gerald.

"Try me," said the man, but he looked more and more doubtful as Gerald told him.

"I knew you wouldn't believe me," Gerald muttered, when he finished.

"Look at it from my position," the man pointed out. "I arrive late at night to take care of a great estate and I find you two trespassing."

"He must be a new caretaker," thought Gerald. "Mabel *lives* here," he told the man quickly. "She's the housekeeper's niece."

"Wherever you live, it's time to go home," the caretaker declared, escorting Gerald to the main gate.

Early the following morning, the children met Mabel and went straight to the temple. The caretaker was sprawled on the ground, knocked out cold.

"Poor man," gasped Cathy. The children clustered around him. He had a cut on his forehead but at least he was breathing. Mabel gently wiped his head.

"Oh dear," said an odd voice. "I hit him with the door when I came out." The children spun around to see an Ugly-Wugly behind them.

Jimmy and Cathy screamed. This Ugly-Wugly looked almost human.

"I found an excellent hotel," it went on. "Shame I lost the others."

"Where are they?" asked Mabel.

"I think they're swimming," it replied. "They left their clothes over there."

A heap of blankets and paper masks was all that remained of the other Ugly-Wuglies. But how had this one become so real? And what could they do with him now?

Just then, the caretaker stirred.

"Please hide!" said Gerald to the Ugly. "A stranger may upset him."

The creature hid behind a bush
as the caretaker sat up.

"I thought- No, it's ridiculous..."

"Are you alright?" asked Mabel.

"I must have tripped," he said,
in a daze, "and you kind children
have looked after me. Thank you,"
he added, struggling to his feet.
"I must go and lie down."

"Whew," said Gerald as he left.
"Now, what-" He broke off
as the Ugly-Wugly
appeared.

"I'm late for
work," it
announced
and strode
away.

"Well, that got rid of him," said Jimmy. "What now?"

"Do you still have the ring?" Mabel asked Gerald. "I think we should put it back before it causes any more trouble."

"It looks innocent enough," said Gerald, handing it over.

"But it isn't," said Cathy. "It's an invisibility ring... I mean a wishing ring... I mean..."

Mabel gave a start. "Suppose it's whatever you *say* it is? And I say it makes you as... as tall as a giant!"

Chapter 5
A midnight feast

As Mabel spoke,
they saw the ring
on her finger,
high above their
heads. She *was*
as tall as a giant,
but had grown no
wider. The effect
was wonderfully
worm-like.

Jimmy's mouth
fell open. "Now
you've done it,"
he said.

"That's right, rub it in," Mabel said bitterly. "It's a wishing ring again," she said, quickly, "and I wish I was normal."

Nothing happened. Mabel stamped a ridiculously long foot.

"Aren't you hungry?" Jimmy asked suddenly. "I am."

"Yes," said Mabel, "and my stomach's so far away. Gerald, will you ask my aunt for a picnic while the others help me hide?"

By the time Mabel was hidden
by the bushes near the stone
dinosaur, Gerald had arrived with
a basket. While they ate, they
discussed the problem of Mabel.

"I have one idea," said Cathy.
"But I won't tell you what in case
it doesn't work. May I take
the ring?"

"Alright," said Mabel.
"Anything's worth a try."

Cathy thought the ring might change its powers if asked by someone not enchanted by it. She climbed into the hollow dinosaur to try her idea in private.

"This *is* a wishing ring," she said, looking around. It was dark inside the dinosaur but wonderfully cool.

"Statues are always cool," she said. "I wish *I* was a statue. Oh!"

Her cry was cut off by a dreadful stony silence. With a sinking heart, Gerald scrambled into the dinosaur and struck a match. There stood Cathy – white and lifeless.

"Somehow the ring's a wishing ring again," Gerald called out to Jimmy and Mabel. "And Cathy went and wished she was a statue."

Jimmy climbed up to see. "Oh wow!" he said.

"Oh no!" said Mabel. "What about the ring? Will you get it, Gerry?"

Gerald thought the ring might have turned to stone too, but it slipped easily off Cathy's cold, smooth marble finger.

Mabel put it on and curled up by the dinosaur. "Will you tell my aunt I'm staying with Cathy tonight?" she asked. "And tell Marie that Cathy's with me."

In the middle of the night, Cathy was woken by tingling in her hands and feet. "The magic's worn off," she thought. She was climbing out of the dinosaur when she felt a jolt. *The dinosaur was moving.*

Cathy jumped down and ran to Mabel. As she shook her awake, Mabel began to shrink. "We can go home," Cathy said delightedly.

"How?" Mabel asked. Cathy was still as white as new-fallen snow. "You're not real yet, you're just a statue come to life."

A cry of "Hello!" broke Cathy's disappointed silence. A statue was smiling at them.

"We're having a midnight feast," he said. "Why don't you join us? You could wish to be a statue too," he added to Mabel, seeing the ring. "Just wish to change back at dawn."

Mabel wished and instantly they were on an island in the lake.

"If only the boys were here," said Cathy, so Mabel wished again. Gerald and Jimmy appeared in their nightshirts, looking shocked. But after explanations and another wish, the boys were statues too.

The party went on until dawn.

At the first rays of the rising sun, the statues vanished and the children were human again. They were also stuck in the middle of the lake – and none of them could swim.

"We need a wish," said Gerald. "Where's the ring?"

Mabel gave a horrified gasp. "I gave it to a statue to look at and... she put it on."

There was a shocked silence.

"The passage from the temple is supposed to lead to this island," said Mabel, "if we can find it."

They found it thanks to Gerald, who tripped over some marble steps.

Leaving the glowing goldness of the sunrise, they went into the underwater passage.

It opened out into a great hall. This hall the children had found was the most beautiful place in the world. The hall was surrounded by arches and through them they saw incredible things.

At the end of the hall was a statue with the ring on her hand.

Cathy took it. "I wish we were all at home in our own beds," she whispered and, at once, they were. (This rather confused Mabel's aunt and Marie. They thought each girl was staying with the other.)

Chapter 6
The Hall of Wishes

A few days later, Mabel called with an invitation. "The caretaker has asked us to a picnic by the stream!"

"But I promised we'd show Marie Yalding Towers," said Gerald. "You three go," he said. "I'll wait for her."

It was a hot day and growing hotter by the minute. When Cathy, Mabel and Jimmy reached the caretaker, they were tired and sticky.

"You need a paddle," he observed.

Dipping their hot feet in cool running water was blissful. And, when they came back, plums and gingerbread were waiting.

"This is as good as our midnight feast," said Jimmy, describing their night with the statues.

The caretaker looked doubtful.

"I'll make you believe me," insisted Jimmy. "Cathy, give him the ring! Now, wish for anything you want."

"There's only one thing I want," he said. "I wish my friend was here."

As he spoke, Marie and Gerald appeared.

"*You!*" said the caretaker.

"*You?*" said Marie, blushing.

"Is she your friend?" asked Cathy.

"Oh yes," said the caretaker, with a wide smile. "Will you excuse us? Marie and I are going for a walk."

Marie sighed. "Yes... Lord Yalding and I have a lot to talk about."

"*He's* Lord Yalding?" said Jimmy.

"Do you think she's the poor girl he loved?" cried Mabel. "And the ring has brought them together?"

There was certainly magic at work. Marie returned from their walk, her eyes sparkling. But Lord Yalding looked a little sad.

"I can't afford to keep the castle any more," he was saying.

"If you're so poor," Jimmy broke in, "why not sell your treasure?"

"Don't be silly," said Lord Yalding. "I don't have any."

"Yes you do," said Jimmy obstinately, and dragged him to the treasure room.

Lord Yalding's face lit up as the jewels were revealed.

"Are there any more secrets in my castle?" he asked.

The children didn't know how to describe the incredible hall, so they took him there too. And, as they stood there, a voice rang out.

"You are in the Hall of Wishes," it said. "The ring has one wish left. The last wish. And that wish is..."

"That all the magic it has done, be undone," said Marie, "and the ring be no more than a plain band of gold to bind me to Lord Yalding for evermore."

The next day, no one remembered what had happened in the hall and the ring was just a gold band. The magic was over so quickly, some of them doubted it had ever happened.

What is certain is that Lord Yalding married Marie and the four children stayed with them every year. And the day after the last wish, this appeared in a newspaper:

Disappearance of city man!
Mr. Ugli, who was a new face in the City, vanished last night, leaving behind only an umbrella, a golf club and a feather duster.

Mr. Ugli was, of course, the Ugly-Wugly who had briefly become real when, in search of a really good hotel, he found himself inside the Hall of Wishes.

FINES
5¢ PER DAY
FOR
OVERDUE BOOKS

E. Nesbit (1858-1924)

Edith Nesbit wrote her
books a hundred years ago,
when most people rode by
horse, not car, and television
hadn't been invented.

   Her stories are full
of excitement and magic.
She wrote *The Enchanted
Castle* in 1907 and the
original book is much longer
and harder to read than this one.
Some of it might seem old-fashioned,
but it's worth trying if you want to know
more about Gerald, Cathy, Jimmy and
Mabel and their other magical adventures.

Designed by Natacha Goransky

Cover design by Russell Punter

First published in 2007 by Usborne Publishing Ltd., Usborne House,
83-85 Saffron Hill, London EC1N 8RT, England. www.usborne.com
Copyright © 2007 Usborne Publishing Ltd. The name Usborne and
the devices ♀ ⊕ are Trade Marks of Usborne Publishing Ltd.
Printed in China U.E. First published in America in 2007